THE UNAUTHORIZED BIOGRAPHY
SCOOP!
ISSUE #10

by Jennifer Poux

Grosset & Dunlap

GROSSET & DUNLAP
An Imprint of Penguin Random House LLC, New York

If you purchased this book without a cover, you should be aware that this book is stolen property. It was reported as "unsold and destroyed" to the publisher, and neither the author nor the publisher has received any payment for this "stripped book."

Penguin supports copyright. Copyright fuels creativity, encourages diverse voices, promotes free speech, and creates a vibrant culture. Thank you for buying an authorized edition of this book and for complying with copyright laws by not reproducing, scanning, or distributing any part of it in any form without permission. You are supporting writers and allowing Penguin to continue to publish books for every reader.

The publisher does not have any control over and does not assume any responsibility for author or third-party websites or their content.

Illustrations by Becky James

Photo credit: cover: Kevin Mazur/WireImage/Getty Images

Copyright © 2021 by Penguin Random House LLC. All rights reserved. Published by Grosset & Dunlap, an imprint of Penguin Random House LLC, New York. GROSSET & DUNLAP is a registered trademark of Penguin Random House LLC. Printed in the USA.

Visit us online at www.penguinrandomhouse.com.

ISBN 9780593224946   10 9 8 7 6 5 4 3 2 1

TABLE OF CONTENTS

●●●●●●●●●●●●●●●●●●●●●●●●●●●

CHAPTER 1: Christmas Tree Farm • 5
   Scoop! Extra: "There's a Monster in My Closet": A Poem by Taylor Swift

   Scoop! Extra: Praying Mantises and Christmas Trees—Really

CHAPTER 2: Wildest Dreams: In Search of Stardom • 16
   Scoop! Extra: Music City, USA

   Scoop! Extra: The Deets on Tay's Debut Album, *Taylor Swift*

CHAPTER 3: Ready for It? A Young Star • 27
   Scoop! Quiz: Match the Lyrics to the *Fearless* Song Titles

CHAPTER 4: Everything Has Changed • 36
   Scoop! Quiz: Taylor Swift, Featuring . . .

CHAPTER 5: Love Stories • 48
   Scoop! Extra: Taylor's Cats

CHAPTER 6: Bad Blood • 57

CHAPTER 7: Miss Americana • 64
   Scoop! Extra: The Chicks

CHAPTER 8: Lover • 74

Scoop! Extra: *Lover's* Easter Eggs

Scoop! Quiz: How Well Do You Know Your *Lover*?

The Ultimate Taylor Swift Quiz

ANSWER KEY • 95

CHAPTER 1

CHRISTMAS TREE FARM

Start with a classic combo: a little girl and a super-sized dream. Add an off-the-charts SCOOP! of songwriting talent and another generous SCOOP! of fierce vocals. Sprinkle on a sparkling smile and brilliant baby blues. Drizzle a coating of that girl-next-door magic. And *bam*!

But don't for a minute think that's all it takes to reach the megastardom of Taylor Swift. This is not some sugarcoated, kitty-unicorn fairy tale—well it is, sort of. But the thing is, Taylor personifies drive, commitment, and hard work. She's been tenacious since she was a kid living in Pennsylvania with her parents, begging to go to Nashville in search of a record deal.

Scoop! Taylor Swift

THE SCOOP! DEETS:

FULL NAME: Taylor Alison Swift
BIRTHDAY: December 13, 1989
BIRTHPLACE: West Reading, Pennsylvania
HEIGHT: 5'11"
INSTAGRAM: 134 million followers
HOMES: New York, Nashville, Los Angeles, Rhode Island
CATS: Meredith Grey, Olivia Benson, Benjamin Button
BOYFRIEND: British actor Joe Alwyn

If you read all the fabulous SCOOP! books (but of course you will) you'll see a theme: Artists aren't born covered in stardust. And they usually don't become household names overnight. That's just not on the regular. The vast majority of them work at it for a long time—like years—before you ever hear their names and know their faces. And Taylor is no exception. But success did come early to her, and that's in part because she knew exactly what she wanted early on.

Taylor set out at eleven years old to make her dreams reality. She had a plan, and with the

Christmas Tree Farm

unwavering support of her parents, she kicked it into action. By the time she turned thirty, Taylor had sold more than fifty million albums!

But let's back up to the beginning. Because this is a story worth telling. And that's what you're here for.

Taylor Swift was born almost two weeks before Christmas on December 13, 1989. Her parents, Andrea and Scott, gave her a gender-neutral name in case she grew up to work in corporate America, like they did.

"My mom thought it was cool that if you got a business card that said 'Taylor' you wouldn't know if it was a guy or a girl," Tay told *Rolling Stone* magazine. "She wanted me to be a business person in a business world."

Here's the SCOOP!
Taylor's parents also named her for the singer James Taylor.

Taylor spent the first decade of her life on her parents' Christmas tree farm in Pennsylvania, riding the family's horses almost as soon as she could walk. (Check out the video for her single "Christmas Tree Farm" for some sweet home movies from that era.) She said it was awesome to have so much space to roam. It's also where she fell in love with the holiday season.

> **In my heart is a Christmas tree farm**
> **Where the people would come**
> **To dance under sparkling lights**
> **Bundled up in their mittens and coats**
> **And the cider would flow**
> **And I just wanna be there tonight**

Her job during Christmas tree season was to pick praying mantis pods off the trees so they wouldn't go home with customers. (See SCOOP! Extra on page 15 for more.)

It didn't hurt that her parents had money—they both worked in finance—so life was pretty cushy on the farm. But her parents gave her a gift more important to her future career than money or a nice house: they let her be a dreamer.

"I had the most magical childhood, running free and going anywhere I wanted to in my head," she told *Rolling Stone*.

She grew up very close to her mom and dad, and still is. "I know I'm so lucky that I got two perfect parents, you know?" Taylor told the *Washington Post* when she was first hitting it big.

Taylor also has a brother, Austin, who came along when she was just over two years old. (Austin is an actor now.) The two blonds grew up on the farm until Taylor was around ten, then the family moved to an even bigger house in Wyomissing, Pennsylvania. Taylor was in fifth grade then.

If you had to guess what kind of student Taylor was, what would you say?

If you said perfectionist, you're right. She was

all about excellent grades and being a good girl. And that comes up over and over again in Taylor's interviews, dating back to when she was a teenager, through adulthood. She was a people pleaser. Sometimes that was a good thing, and it worked in her favor—and sometimes it wasn't so great. (More on that later!) Regardless of the pros and cons, it was how she was built.

Taylor was also a romantic with a colorful imagination. She rode horses competitively, but she says being so tall made her awkward and gawky, and she wasn't cut out for team sports. (You gotta think the basketball and volleyball coaches wanted her with that height, right?) Anyway, it wasn't sports that took up space in her brain. It was the stories she wrote. She preferred poetry and singing along to LeAnn Rimes CDs to hoops, which didn't sit well with the other kids in her class.

Even if it wasn't always the cool thing to do, according to her classmates, Taylor stayed true to her interests. In fifth grade she entered a national poetry contest with a poem about a monster in her closet—and won! The poem was published in an anthology, and even her class thought that was pretty amazing. (See SCOOP! Extra on page 13 for the actual poem.)

It was around this time that Taylor dove into musical theater. She first got the acting bug in a school play and auditioned for the Berks County Youth Theatre Academy. First show: *Annie*. She played one of the orphans. Even though she had a small role, Taylor stood out from the cast, and it wasn't just because she was so much taller than the other girls. She had mad stage presence, and of course, the pipes. The director saw that Taylor was a natural, and he never cast her in a small role again. During her time with the theater company, Taylor played Maria in *The Sound of Music*, Sandy in *Grease*, and Kim MacAfee in *Bye Bye Birdie*. (Had to be some jealous actresses in that company, right?)

It was also around this time that her passion for

country music took hold. It's not like she lived in a place where kids listened to country. But she was all in for Shania Twain, the Chicks, and LeAnn Rimes. (She got her first LeAnn Rimes CD when she was just six.) She started trying to sing like her favorite artists. And at some point, she realized she was more into singing than acting.

LeAnn Rimes hit it big at thirteen, and Taylor figured she could, too.

"THERE'S A MONSTER IN MY CLOSET" A POEM BY TAYLOR SWIFT

There's a monster in my closet and I don't know what to do!
Have you ever seen him?
Has he ever pounced on you?
I wonder what he looks like!
Is he purple with red eyes?
I wonder what he likes to eat.
What about his size!!
Tonight I'm gonna catch him!
I'll set a real big trap!
Then I'll train him really well.
He'll answer when I clap!

When I looked up in that closet, there was nothing there but stuff.
I know that monster's in there!
I heard him huff and puff!
Could it be he wants to eat me?
Maybe I'm his favorite tray.

And if he comes to get me,
I'll scream loudly, "Go away!!"
If he's nice, I'll name him "Happy."
If he's bad I'll name him "Grouch."
I suspect that he is leaving, but if not . . .
    I'll kick him out!

PRAYING MANTISES AND CHRISTMAS TREES—REALLY

It just sounded so weird: Taylor was supposed to check all the Christmas trees on the farm for praying mantis egg pods before they were sold. So we had to do a little research. And it is a thing. Though it is fairly rare, praying mantises sometimes lay their eggs in evergreen trees—they apparently prefer the Fraser fir variety. So if you see something that looks like a walnut-sized pine cone attached to a branch of your Christmas tree, just clip it off and put it outside. If the eggs hatch in your house, you could have an invasion of one hundred to two hundred baby praying mantises! Could be a little freaky. And they'll starve inside.

CHAPTER 2

WILDEST DREAMS: IN SEARCH OF STARDOM

Before she played piano and guitar, Taylor Swift liked to sing to karaoke music—country tunes, of course. So when she decided it was time to chase her dreams in the country music capital of the world, Nashville, Tennessee, Taylor recorded a demo CD with four tracks set to karaoke music: Dolly Parton's "Here You Come Again," "There's Your Trouble" by the Chicks, "One Way Ticket" by LeAnn Rimes, and one outlier: "Hopelessly Devoted to You" from *Grease*. On the front of the CD case was Taylor's headshot—on the back, her phone number.

With Austin in the backseat, Taylor and her mom took a road trip over spring break to Nashville where the bubbly and optimistic eleven-year-old went door-to-door on Music Row, handing her demo to the receptionists at some twenty record companies. (That takes some serious courage.) The people she met thought she was cute but didn't take her seriously. Some told her to come back when she was eighteen. But she still had LeAnn Rimes's story in her head. She wasn't going to wait until she was eighteen to make a record.

Taylor didn't return to Pennsylvania with any record deals. But one of the producers did call the number on her CD. He told her she had a good voice, and she was cute—but she needed to sing original songs.

It was a blow. But it may have been the best advice she ever got.

Taylor started taking guitar lessons and her teacher helped her write her first song, "Lucky You." She'd always been a poet, and she loved to write. It made sense. Her parents bought her the twelve-string guitar she wanted and soon helped her find a manager who could kick-start her career.

Taylor performed on the weekends in local

Scoop! Taylor Swift

festivals and contests, and she sang at the Pat Garrett Roadhouse in a weekly karaoke contest. "I sang every single week for a year and a half until I won," she told *Rolling Stone*. (The prize was opening for the Charlie Daniels Band. She played at 10:30 a.m.—he played at 8:30 p.m.)

Taylor wasn't interested in playing sports, but she liked playing sports arenas. In April 2002, she belted out "The Star-Spangled Banner" at the Philadelphia 76ers NBA Finals game. Twenty thousand people were there! She was just twelve years old, wearing a red, white, and blue flag dress, a red cardigan sweater, and a matching red headband in her long, wavy blond hair. A sweet little girl with a booming, soulful voice. She looks so comfortable in the video—like she's been doing it forever. (Check it out on YouTube!)

> **Here's the SCOOP! When she walked off the court, she got a high five from Jay-Z! He told her that her singing was beautiful.**

Wildest Dreams: In Search of Stardom

When Taylor was thirteen, she performed some of her dozens of original songs in an RCA Records showcase. RCA, a major record company, liked her so much they gave her an artistic development deal. And she and her mom started traveling down to Nashville pretty often. The dream was starting to take shape.

Ever the supportive father figure, Taylor's dad transferred to an office in Nashville (what a guy!), and the family moved to a house on a lake in Hendersonville, Tennessee, when Taylor was fourteen. That's where she went to high school for a while, and where she met her best friend, Abigail Anderson, freshman year in English class, when they were fifteen. (You know the song.)

Taylor landed a sweet job in Nashville in addition to the RCA development deal: a writing gig with Sony. She'd go to the studios after school to write songs and work with some of Sony's professional songwriters. She loved writing music, but she was getting frustrated—she wanted to make an album.

Instead, people kept telling her she was too young. In a risky move, she decided to cut RCA loose.

But she continued to write for Sony and one of its seasoned writers, Liz Rose, invited her to sing at the Bluebird Café in Nashville one night. Taylor performed a short acoustic set of her own songs to a packed room, and when she finished, a man approached her with his business card: It was record producer Scott Borchetta. Right there at the Bluebird he held an impromptu meeting with Taylor and her parents, telling them he was about to start his own company: Big Machine Records. And he wanted her to come record for him. Taylor had a good feeling about Borchetta right away, and once he committed to letting her sing her own songs, she said yes to his offer.

Borchetta opened Big Machine Records and gave Taylor the freedom to make a record of her own songs. She wrote three of the tracks on her album *Taylor Swift* alone, and the other eight she cowrote with Rose and other writers. In October

2006, she finally released her first album. She may not have been thirteen like LeAnn Rimes, but she was only sixteen and still in high school. Pretty amazing. The album was a hit. (See SCOOP! Extra on page 26 for more.)

And Taylor's social life was getting a bump at her new school. For one thing, she had a bestie now: Abigail. For another, she had a boyfriend: Brandon Borello. He was a cute senior when she was a freshman, and that was the one downside: He graduated while they were still going out, and they broke up when he went off to college.

Another upside to life at Hendersonville High: The kids didn't think country music was wack. Just about everyone was into it. But as in her middle school in Pennsylvania, Taylor felt she wasn't popular. She told *Rolling Stone*, "There were queen bees and attendants, and I was maybe the friend of one of the attendants. I was the girl who didn't get invited to parties, but if I did happen to go, you know, no one would throw a bottle at my head."

Phew! A bottle to the head? No thanks.

Taylor wasn't into drinking or smoking or generally doing any of the rebellious things teens often do. She said she never wanted to disappoint her parents, and she was big on image. She wanted young girls to look up to her, and parents to feel good about it.

She was still an academic overachiever in high school—Taylor had a 4.0 average. She stayed at Hendersonville High freshman and sophomore year; she was homeschooled in junior and senior year to make time for her career. She finished the coursework for both grades in just twelve months, graduating a year early!

Tay didn't go to prom at her high school because, as she told the *Washington Post*, "As supportive as my hometown is, in my high school there are people who would probably walk up to me and punch me in the face. There's a select few that will never like me. They don't like what I stand for. They don't like somebody who stands for being sober, who stands for anything happy. They're going to be negative no matter what. I've had people tell me it would be a security issue if I went back to prom."

Eventually Taylor did go to prom, in a tour bus on TV. In MTV's *Once upon a Prom*, the famous eighteen-year-old Taylor Swift went to prom—at Hillcrest High School in Tuscaloosa, Alabama. Taylor chose Whit Wright out of fifty dateless Hillcrest seniors who sent MTV videos. And she brought Abigail. At the time, Taylor told *People* magazine, "It was literally one of the best nights of my life!" Must have been pretty lit for Whit, too.

> **Here's a double SCOOP! Taylor changed out of her prom dress into a pink one from her tour bus when Whit said he was wearing a pink vest for a family friend who had breast cancer.**

MUSIC CITY, USA

What's so slammin' about Nashville, you ask? It's the country music capital of the United States, otherwise known as Music City. It's where dreams are realized, and stars are born. There are more than fifty-five thousand music jobs in Nashville, a city of fewer than 770,000 people! So if you want to be a music producer, it's a good place to give it a shot. Nashville's competitors in the music industry—Los Angeles, New York, and London—are much bigger cities.

This Tennessee city is unique, and so is its music history. In the late 1800s, Ryman Auditorium became one of the country's premier performing spaces due to its superior acoustics. From 1925 to 1974, it was home to the Grand Ole Opry, a weekly country music concert on the radio. In 1950, Nashville was officially dubbed Music City,

USA, by a radio announcer, David Cobb of WSM. The name has stuck ever since. There are a number of other renowned music venues in Nashville, including Tennessee Performing Arts Center, Mercy Lounge, and the Bluebird Café, where Taylor Swift got her start. And many a county music star has found fame in this southern city with a national reputation for producing some of the country's most popular music.

SCOOP! EXTRA

THE DEETS ON TAY'S
⬇ DEBUT ALBUM, *TAYLOR SWIFT* ⬇

- 💜 Five singles were released off the album. The first, "Tim McGraw," reached the top ten on *Billboard*'s Hot Country Songs. All five singles have been certified platinum or multiplatinum.

- 💜 "Tim McGraw" is about her high school boyfriend, Brandon Borello, who was graduating when Taylor was a freshman and wrote the song.

- 💜 The single "Teardrops on My Guitar" was about her high school friend Drew, on whom she had a crush.

- 💜 *Taylor Swift* was the longest charting album on the *Billboard* 200 of the 2000s, staying on the chart for a whopping 277 weeks!

- 💜 Taylor promoted the album by opening for artists Tim McGraw and Faith Hill, Rascal Flatts, George Strait, and Brad Paisley.

- 💜 Taylor wrote the single "Our Song" for her high school talent show, not intending to include it on the album. It made Swift the youngest person to write and perform a number-one song on the Hot Country Songs chart.

CHAPTER 3

READY FOR IT? A YOUNG STAR

A few months after *Once upon a Prom*, Taylor released *Fearless*, an album all about life and love in high school. It was dope! "Love Story," the first single, peaked at number four on the *Billboard* Hot 100 and hit number one in Australia. It sold more than eighteen million copies worldwide, making it one of the best-selling singles of all time! Not bad for a teenager.

> **Here's the SCOOP!** "Love Story" went to number one on *Billboard*'s Top Country and Pop charts, the first song ever to do that!

Those are just stats. You can't overestimate the

impact of this song on Taylor's career. I mean, come on—for many of a certain age, "Love Story" is one of the *it* Taylor Swift songs. Even if you weren't born yet, you know it: Those dreamy teenage-girl lyrics, the video with its soft focus and fairy-tale ball gowns, and Taylor's sweet voice. It all added up to a confection of perfection. And it sold an idea and an ideal to teenage girls who wanted to be Taylor—and wanted to fall in love.

> We were both young when I first saw you
> I close my eyes, and the flashback starts
> I'm standing there
> On a balcony in summer air

Taylor says she was in the throes of a *Romeo and Juliet* scenario in her own life—her parents thought the boy she liked was a creep—which inspired her to write the song. But she decided to take Shakespeare's quintessential tragic love story and turn it on its head.

"If that had just gone a little bit differently, it could have been the best love story ever told. And it is one of the best love stories ever told, but it's a tragedy," she said during an interview with the *Los Angeles Times*. "I thought, why can't you . . . make it a happy ending and put a key change in the song and turn it into a marriage proposal?"

> Here's a little **SCOOP!** Taylor says she keeps a piano near her just about all the time so she can write when inspiration hits.

Killer move, Taylor. And it proved something to the recording industry: there was a big market of young girls waiting to buy records they could relate to, something Taylor had been telling anyone who would listen since she was eleven.

Four more singles were released: "White Horse," "Fifteen," "Fearless," and "You Belong With Me," which hit the number two slot on *Billboard*

Scoop! Taylor Swift

Hot 100. This is the track that for so many is *the* Taylor Swift song. The video for "You Belong With Me" won Taylor an award at the MTV Video Music Awards in 2009—her acceptance speech infamously interrupted by Kanye West. (More on that later!) Check it out: That video has more than over a billion views! Whaaaat?

Talk about a song that's relatable for teen girls. She wrote it after overhearing a male friend arguing with his girlfriend on the phone. Most moms of that era will remember these lyrics:

> But she wears short skirts
> I wear T-shirts
> She's cheer captain
> And I'm on the bleachers
> Dreaming about the day when you wake up
> And find that what you're looking for has been here the whole time

In the video, Taylor plays both a popular girl and a nerd dreaming of the popular girl's boyfriend. Brilliant.

Did you know the *Fearless* song "Forever & Always" was a late-add to the album? It's about Joe Jonas and their pretty public breakup. She announced that one on *The Ellen DeGeneres Show*, one of many appearances she would make on the show over the years.

Ellen asks her if the title is sarcastic. "Definitely," she says. (More on that later!)

The accolades kept coming: five American Music Awards, and *Fearless* won Album of the Year and Best Country Album at the Grammys, just two of the four Grammy awards Taylor won that year. The crossover from country to pop was underway. Taylor was becoming a phenomenon. And *Fearless* was the best-selling album of 2009 in the United States.

It wasn't all sunlight and rainbows for Taylor. While sales of *Fearless* were making her rich, there were critics (always!) who said it was an anti-feminist album. Some people said Lady Gaga should have won the Grammy for Album of the Year. That Swift was overrated. She was just a country singer. There was the dustup with Kanye and all the fallout. It was the beginning of what Taylor would face throughout her career: the constant interplay of huge success and very loud criticism.

But loads of offers came Taylor's way during and after her second album's success. Collaborations with people like John Mayer and Kellie Pickler, her first film role, in *Valentine's Day*, and credits on that soundtrack for two songs. She also cowrote two songs for the *Hannah Montana: The Movie* soundtrack. A guest slot on *CSI* as a rebellious teen. And then *Saturday Night Live* invited her to host and be the musical guest. If you haven't watched it, check out her opening musical monologue. She sang a song about what she's not going to sing about in her monologue, including this reference to Joe Jonas and their recent breakup:

"Hey Joe, I'm doing real well, tonight I'm hosting *SNL*, but I'm not going to brag about that, in my monologue." (Queen!)

Ready for It? A Young Star

Then she sang that she wasn't going to comment on a certain werewolf, but whispered, "Hi, Taylor," winked, and blew him a kiss.

And then she had fun with a certain interrupter. "You might be expecting me to say something bad about Kanye, and how he ran up on the stage and ruined my VMA monologue . . ."

The monologue and her subsequent skits proved that Taylor can be hilarious. Her appearances on *Ellen* are funny. Maybe this is Taylor Swift's most underrated attribute: She has a sharp sense of humor and good comic timing. The fact that she could laugh off the controversies that swirled around her as an eighteen-year-old thrust into the public eye: savage.

SCOOP! QUIZ

MATCH THE LYRICS TO THE *FEARLESS* SONG TITLES:

1. Never a clean break, no one here to save me
2. I want to stay right here in this passenger's seat
3. Count to ten, take it in
4. I don't know who I'm gonna talk to now at school
5. So I've got some things to say to you
6. And I was crying on the staircase
7. And I stare at the phone, he still hasn't called
8. This ain't Hollywood, this is a small town
9. And you might think I'm bulletproof, but I'm not
10. I'm the one who makes you laugh

A. "YOU BELONG WITH ME"
B. "WHITE HORSE"
C. "FEARLESS"
D. "LOVE STORY"
E. "HEY STEPHEN"
F. "FOREVER & ALWAYS"
G. "THE BEST DAY"
H. "FIFTEEN"
I. "BREATHE"
J. "TELL ME WHY"

Ready for It? A Young Star

How did you do?

1-3 correct: Pop those headphones on!

4-7 correct: You're rusty, Swiftie!

7-10 correct: This is a Love Story.

Check your answers on page 95!

CHAPTER 4

EVERYTHING HAS CHANGED

*W*ith albums, come tours. And with tours, comes a grueling schedule and life on the road. But that didn't stop Taylor from putting out a third album, *Speak Now*. She wrote the whole darn thing, in all its country/pop glory. There's still an undeniably country sound on this album, but the shift to pop is getting real.

The lead track, "Mine," is about someone, or more than one guy—she never names him. But it's a good introduction to this collection about love and regret and broken hearts: country themes with pop twists.

Speak Now has at least two songs that address ex-boyfriends. "Dear John" is about John Mayer. At nearly seven minutes long, it's the longest song on the album and the longest one she's recorded to date. (That must mean something.) And "Back to December" is apparently an apology to Taylor Lautner after their breakup.

And, of course, there's "Mean," a song directed at her critics. In a *60 Minutes* interview she said it was actually aimed at a critic who trashed her performance at the 52nd Grammy Awards when she sang off-key with Stevie Nicks. The writer said her career was over.

"I don't have thick skin," she has said. But fortunately for her fans, she has an uncanny talent for turning heartache into lyrics. And even though these lyrics are based on her own personal experiences and few of her fans are celebs, she still manages to touch a chord in millions of people with just about every song she pens. And she does it without going to some deep, dark place.

Even after reaching the age of twenty-one, a time when some stars go in an entirely different direction to prove they're adults, Taylor kept her image clean and youthful. She didn't do anything stupid or get arrested or caught doing drugs.

"I definitely think about a million people when I'm getting dressed in the morning. That's just part of my life now," she told *60 Minutes* back in 2011. "It would be really easy to say, I'm twenty-one now, I do what I want. You raise your kids. But that's not the truth of it. The truth of it is that every single singer out there with songs on the radio is raising the next generation. So make your words count." That's heavy.

There weren't a lot of other stars living by that credo, so major kudos to Taylor for recognizing who her fans are and being a role model for them.

The global, seventy-six-city tour to promote *Speak Now* included aerialists and fireworks, quick wardrobe changes and complicated entrances, and screaming girls. Always screaming teenage girls. If you haven't been to a Taylor Swift concert, just know it gets loud! For her young fans, Taylor's songs have provided a life soundtrack. And they know all the words.

One of the cool things about Taylor's tours is that she always sets aside time before and after the show to meet and greet lucky fans. And she makes sure to sing to the fans stuck in the back of the venue. Her crew looks for enthusiastic fans throughout an arena to give them access to her after the concerts.

Every choice Taylor makes with the tour is based on her own experiences going to concerts as a kid. "There's no way to guarantee everyone a front-row seat in a stadium but we do the closest we possibly can by moving the stage and moving me, and having me fly over them," she told Elvis Duran on his radio show in 2019 during the *Lover* tour.

Taylor makes sick money on those tours—selling out huge arenas and her concert merch. But it's a ton of work. And ever since the terrorist attack on an Ariana Grande concert in England, it's caused Tay a ton of stress. She says stadium tours have turned into her greatest fear. How can she and her team keep millions of people safe? She says they

Scoop! Taylor Swift

spend an enormous amount of time and money to prevent such an attack and protect her fans and crew.

It's not just on tour that Taylor has to worry about safety. There are some creepers out there—some stans who are downright scary.

> **Here's the SCOOP!** "I carry QuikClot army grade bandage dressing, which is for gunshot or stab wounds," she wrote in *Elle*.

"Websites and tabloids have taken it upon themselves to post every home address I've ever had online." (That is messed up.) "You get enough stalkers trying to break into your house and you kind of start prepping for bad things," she wrote in an essay for *Elle* when she was turning thirty. While they were recording "ME!" she told Brendon Urie of Panic! at the Disco that once a guy slept in her bed at one of her apartments when she wasn't home! That could really freak you out.

Mega celebrity makes it almost impossible to step outside your own home without paparazzi and fans waiting for you. It might sound glam, but it's not a fun part of the job. Especially all these years later. There's a scene in the documentary *Miss Americana* when Taylor's getting into a limo outside her New York City apartment, and there are rows of fans waiting for her on the sidewalk, like they're lining up to get into a nightclub. She says in the movie she's quite aware of how abnormal that is.

But the flip side is that she still manages to connect one-on-one with her fans. You know, those album preview parties (secret sessions) at her homes, where she bakes and invites strangers into her living room? "I want to come up with as many ways that we can spend time together and bond because it keeps me normal. It keeps my life feeling manageable."

After *Speak Now* came *Red*, and a transition to

the pop world. That album included collaborations with Ed Sheeran and Gary Lightbody of Snow Patrol. The album debuted at number one on *Billboard* 200, her third consecutive number-one album. It also made her the first female artist to have two consecutive two-million album openings.

"We Are Never Ever Getting Back Together"—remember that one? Reportedly about Jake Gyllenhaal, you gotta love how up-tempo this post-breakup song is.

> **Then you come around again and say**
> **"Baby, I miss you and I swear I'm gonna change, trust me"**
> **Remember how that lasted for a day?**
> **I say, "I hate you," we break up, you call me, "I love you"**

So familiar to anyone whose breakup didn't stick the first time. There are other great songs on *Red*, but we're skipping ahead to 2014, and the release of *1989*, named for Taylor's birth year.

Some stats: *1989* won the Grammy for Album of the Year, making her the first woman to win that award twice. First week sales: 1.287 million—made her the first artist to have three million-selling albums within the first week of release in the country. *1989* has sold 6.2 million copies in the US and 10.1 million copies worldwide.

This is what she said onstage when she won that Grammy: "To all the young women out there, there are going to be people along the way who will try to undercut your success or take credit for your accomplishments or your fame, but if you just focus on the work and you don't let those people sidetrack you, someday when you get where you're going, you'll look around and you will know that it was you, and the people who love you that put you there."

It was a tougher, older, more feminist Taylor Swift emerging that night. Still every bit the role model—maybe even more so.

"Blank Space," "Bad Blood," "Shake It Off," "Welcome to New York," "1989." There's no more country in the album; she had moved to New York City and was making big changes in her music and her life. The songs are still about relationships ("Blank Space") and friendships ("Bad Blood") and her critics ("Shake It Off") but the sound is entirely pop, marked by synthesizers and studio percussion.

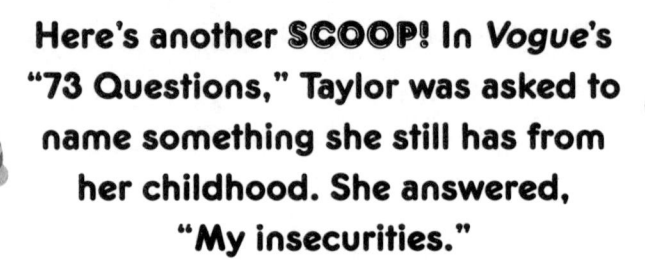

> Here's another SCOOP! In *Vogue*'s "73 Questions," Taylor was asked to name something she still has from her childhood. She answered, "My insecurities."

With "Bad Blood" especially, *1989* gives you the sense that Taylor was not only shedding her country vibe, but also those childhood insecurities. She had her friends in The Squad, as her friendships with Selena Gomez, Lena Dunham, and models like Karlie Kloss and Gigi Hadid were known. No more unpopular girl. And she was shaking off feuds (more on that later!), standing up for herself, and trying to look past the years of commentary on her love life.

> 'Cause the players gonna play, play, play, play, play
> And the haters gonna hate, hate, hate, hate, hate
> Baby, I'm just gonna shake, shake, shake, shake, shake
> I shake it off, I shake it off

More about Taylor's love life and the people who mean the most to her, next.

SCOOP! QUIZ

TAYLOR SWIFT, FEATURING . . .

Match the singers to the Taylor Swift song that features them!

1. PAULA FERNANDES
2. THE CIVIL WARS
3. ZAYN
4. ED SHEERAN AND FUTURE
5. GARY LIGHTBODY
6. BRENDON URIE
7. BON IVER
8. ED SHEERAN
9. KENDRICK LAMAR
10. SHAWN MENDES

A. "LOVER"
B. "END GAME"
C. "THE LAST TIME"
D. "SAFE & SOUND"
E. "ME!"
F. "I DON'T WANNA LIVE FOREVER"
G. "BAD BLOOD"
H. "EXILE"
I. "LONG LIVE"
J. "EVERYTHING HAS CHANGED"

Everything Has Changed

How did you do?

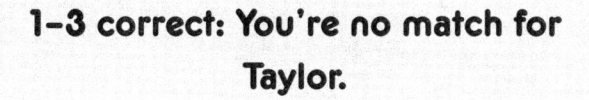

1-3 correct: You're no match for Taylor.

4-7 correct: You're a wannabe collaborator.

8-10 correct: You're ready for your duet!

Check your answers on page 95!

CHAPTER 5

LOVE STORIES

When you're as famous and as gorgeous and glam as Taylor Swift, and your dates are as famous and glam as Harry Styles and Tom Hiddleston, your love life makes headlines. But in the case of Taylor Swift, her love life has been dissected and ridiculed and talked about for years—more than the average celebrity.

For a few years it was way over the top—and wrong. She was a young woman in her twenties having fun, dating, meeting new people, doing what twenty-somethings do. If she were a man??? But tabloids and other media outlets called her on it over and over again—as if what she was doing was illegal, or immoral.

Now that she's been in a committed relationship

with Joe Alwyn (as of this writing) for more than three years, you hear very little about her love life. And that's mostly because Tay and Joe want it that way—they are super private. But it's also because the media got bored—one man, one relationship, doesn't interest them.

They weren't bored back in 2016, in the wake of Tay's back-to-back album successes and rising global fame. At a small concert at the GRAMMY Museum that year, Taylor played "Blank Space"—just her voice and an acoustic guitar—explaining what had prompted her to write it.

"In the last couple of years, the media have had a really wonderful fixation on kind of painting me as like the psycho-serial-dater girl. It's been awesome. I've loved it." Sarcasm, of course.

She says that, at first, all the negative attention bummed her out. But then she realized the media had created an interesting character, one that didn't resemble her: a girl who jet sets around the world collecting men. She can get any of them but she's

Scoop! Taylor Swift

so clingy that they leave. And in the "Blank Space" video, you see her playing that role, mocking the critics.

Instead of attacking her, you could look at Taylor as having been lucky to date some hot, talented, and (sometimes) cool guys. And some of them gave her great material:

"Forever & Always" is about Joe Jonas. And she told Ellen first about how he broke up with her.

"When I find that person that, that is right for me, he'll be wonderful. And when I look at that person, I'm not even going to be able to remember the boy who broke up with me over the phone in twenty-five seconds when I was eighteen." Ellen looks stunned. "No, [he] did not!" Yes, he did.

> **Here's the SCOOP!** Later she told Ellen that calling Joe out was the most rebellious thing she did as a teenager.

"We Are Never Ever Getting Back Together" is

supposedly about Jake Gyllenhaal. They went out for a few months.

"Style"—got to be Harry Styles, right? "I Knew You Were Trouble" is about Harry, too.

John Mayer was not happy she wrote "Dear John" about him. Oh well.

Too old (John), too young (that Kennedy boy), too unreliable (Jake.) There were other men and songs. But it seems she's found her Goldilocks man in Joe Alwyn—just right.

HERE ARE THE DEETS ON JOE ALWYN:

- ♥ He's a British actor.
- ♥ He was born in 1991, so just a bit younger.
- ♥ Ed Sheeran approves of him.
- ♥ He was in the films *Harriet* and *The Favourite*.
- ♥ They may have met at the 2016 Met Gala.

Neither Joe nor Taylor posts photos of the other on their Instagrams, but they posted a photo of the

Scoop! Taylor Swift

same cactus on the same day. His shot was of him and the cactus; her shot was of her with the cactus. A crumb to be sure, but still a crumb. They were cuddly at the 2020 Golden Globes. But mostly, they stay away from the cameras. Smart.

Love and its pursuit have been constants in Taylor's life and song catalog. But there are only a few people who have provided consistent unconditional love from the beginning. Abigail has remained her friend since ninth grade. If you watch *Miss Americana*, you will see how even today, Taylor's mother, Andrea, is so important in her life and always has been.

"My mom is my best friend. She's been there for me when no one else has. And she's never been afraid of telling me the honest truth."

Not to leave out her dad. She loves him dearly and says he is a big teddy bear.

> **Here's a fatherly SCOOP! You can find Scott Swift in the "The Man" video.**

Love Stories

Whether she's deciding to dive into politics, or just needs a companion on her tour plane, Tay's mother is very present in her life.

Sadly, Andrea was diagnosed with cancer. And then she relapsed while Taylor was filming the documentary *Miss Americana*. And while she was undergoing treatment, doctors found a brain tumor.

As anyone can understand, it was devastating for Taylor and her family. And she wrote a song about it, a song that's different from anything she's written before. The lyrics are heartbreaking and universal to anyone who has ever witnessed a loved one's struggle with cancer.

> **The buttons of my coat were tangled in my hair**
> **In doctor's-office lighting, I didn't tell you I was scared**
> **That was the first time we were there**
> **Holy orange bottles, each night I pray to you**
> **Desperate people find faith, so now I pray to Jesus, too**

Taylor cut short her *Lover* tour so she could be with her mom. Her mom's illness is something she doesn't talk about much in interviews because it is, understandably, too difficult.

SCOOP! EXTRA

TAYLOR'S CATS

If you know anything about Taylor Swift, you know how she feels about cats. (Kitty backpack with a window, anyone?) Taylor's got three. The two cats she's had the longest are Dr. Meredith Grey (named for the lead character in *Grey's Anatomy*) and Olivia Benson (named for a character in *Law & Order: Special Victims Unit*.) Both of them are Scottish Folds which have a genetic mutation that causes their ears to fold down. Her third cat is Benjamin Button (named for Brad Pitt's character in *The Curious Case of Benjamin Button*). Benjamin is a Ragdoll that was in her video for the single "ME!" off the *Lover* album. Taylor says a woman brought the kitten to the set and handed him to her, and that was that. "He just starts purring and he looks at me like, 'You're my mom, and we're going to live together.'" She says she instantly fell in love. The kitten didn't have a home yet. Of course she had to adopt him. Lucky Benjamin!

CHAPTER 6

BAD BLOOD

There's an American tradition of building artists up and turning them into world-famous celebrities, only to tear them down and revel in their misery (brutal, huh?). Some people love to watch the mighty crash. And social media has made a sport of canceling celebrities.

If you're a Swiftie, you know she's been subjected to that kind of seesaw attention for years. Up one day, down the next. America's sweetheart on Monday, an evil, manipulative backstabber by Friday. But there's one thing that makes her stand out and above all the hateful noise: Taylor Swift has never really fallen. She's been beaten up on social media, and she's dropped out of the public eye when the heat came too close, but she keeps getting back up and killing it, making hit records. (The best revenge is living well, right?)

Taylor is the first to admit she's made mistakes. (Who hasn't?) But since she was a little girl dreaming of success, she's worked hard to be a role model. Is that sweet girl-next-door image real? The haters like to say it isn't. She's fake—who could be that nice, that good? But remember: she was always a people pleaser. She wants to be liked and respected. (Who doesn't?) With Taylor, it was a guiding principle.

"My entire moral code as a kid and now is a need to be thought of as good. Do the right thing, do the good thing. And obviously I'm not a perfect person by any stretch, but overall, the main thing that I always tried to be was just like a good girl," she says in the documentary *Miss Americana*.

So how does she deal with the negativity?

She sings about it, of course. From "Mean" to "Bad Blood," to songs about her exes, Taylor exacts artistic revenge when she's feeling particularly put upon. And she vows to continue on that path.

"When they stop coming for me, I will stop singing to them," she told *CBS Sunday Morning*.

"People go on and on about, like, you have to forgive and forget to move past something. No you don't. You don't have to forgive and you don't have to forget to move on." That's a woman speaking from experience.

But Taylor wasn't always so dismissive and philosophical about the haters. She's internalized the criticism, and when it's coming from every angle that can be tough to get past.

"People love a hate frenzy. It's like piranhas. People had so much fun hating me, and they didn't really need very many reasons to do it," she told *Rolling Stone* in 2019. "And I couldn't figure out how to learn from it. Because I wasn't sure exactly what I did that was so wrong."

See what happened there? She said she couldn't figure out what she was doing wrong. It didn't occur to Taylor when she was younger that maybe what she was doing wrong was being successful at everything she did. Sometimes that's all it takes for the haters to unleash the dogs.

She says she was like a golden retriever, revealing everything to anyone who asked. Happy to chat. And too ready to listen to the noise.

"Since I was fifteen years old, if people criticized me for something, I changed it," she told *Rolling Stone*. "When I was eighteen, they were like, 'She doesn't really write those songs.' So my third album I wrote by myself as a reaction to that. Then they decided I was a serial dater—a boy-crazy man-eater—when I was twenty-two. And so I didn't date anyone for, like, two years. And then they decided in 2016 that absolutely everything about me was wrong. If I did something good, it was for the wrong reasons. If I did something brave, I didn't do it correctly. If I stood up for myself, I was throwing a tantrum. And so I found myself in this endless mockery echo chamber."

That's some serious pressure!

Bad Blood

And then there were the celebrity feuds, bookended by Kanye West.

What should have been a poppin' moment in Taylor's career blew up into one of the worst and most infamous moments in music award history. If you haven't seen it, check out the video from the 2009 MTV VMA awards. Taylor had just received the award for best female music video for "You Belong With Me" when Kanye jumped onstage, grabbed a mic, and said, "Yo, Taylor, I'm really happy for you. I'mma let you finish, but Beyoncé had one of the best videos of all time" (for "Single Ladies [Put a Ring on It]". More on this feud in chapter 7!

> **Here's the SCOOP!** Turns out P!nk came to Taylor's defense, giving Kanye a piece of her mind during the commercial break.

Another celebrity feud that got some serious

Scoop! Taylor Swift

media attention: the fight between Taylor and Katy Perry. The two singers, once friends, had a dispute over the hiring of some backup dancers. Not that interesting. But a great Taylor Swift song came out of this one: "Bad Blood," featuring Kendrick Lamar, with a killer video that stars Lena Dunham, Selena Gomez, Karlie Kloss, and Mariska Hargitay. She never admitted the song was about Katy, but that's the general consensus. Then Katy responded with "Swish Swish" and an accompanying video. And people think it's about Taylor.

This is another fight that went on forever, if anybody really cared. But it seems to have been resolved. Check out Taylor's star-studded video for "You Need to Calm Down" off the *Lover* album. Katy makes an appearance as a hamburger who hugs it out with Taylor, dressed as french fries.

Both women saw the concept for the video as a good way to be models of civility. In a BBC interview, Taylor said, "I sent it to her and she said, 'I would love for us to be a symbol of redemption and forgiveness!'" And they decided it wasn't enough to be a symbol: They really wanted to mend fences. So they got together and talked for hours.

Nice going, ladies!

> **Here's the double SCOOP!** Taylor says the hamburger/fries embrace is really a comment on how the media loves to pit women against each other.

CHAPTER 7

MISS AMERICANA

As it turns out, that cringy Kanye moment at the 2009 VMAs was more impactful than anyone could have guessed. In the 2019 *Miss Americana* documentary on Netflix, Taylor says, "For someone who's built their whole belief system on getting people to clap for you, the whole crowd booing is a pretty formative experience."

Remember, she was still just a teenager and still making her way as a country singer. The VMAs were a big deal, an important evening in the pop world—a place she didn't feel comfortable in just yet. And even though the crowd was actually booing Kanye, she thought they were booing her. (So awful!) Think about how you'd feel if someone at school called you out in front of a class or the cafeteria or on social media. Then multiply it by millions of people watching.

In *Miss Americana*, Taylor says that moment messed her up. "That was, like, sort of a catalyst for a lot of psychological paths that I went down. And not all of them were beneficial."

It also marked the beginning of a timeline of big successes for Taylor Swift, with many more awards shows and statuettes. Kanye didn't stop her; if anything, he helped fuel her drive. In the next five-plus years, Taylor became a beloved superstar.

But the Kanye West mess didn't disappear, either. And when she was in her midtwenties, Kanye worked it. With the release of his song "Famous," in which he called Taylor the b-word, and with the fallout that followed, Taylor was on the receiving end of serious negative press and a lot of hate. Next thing she knew, #TaylorSwiftIsOverParty was the number-one trending Twitter hashtag worldwide.

Taylor couldn't bounce back from all the hate, and she disappeared from the public eye for about a year. She says when people fall out of love with you, there's nothing you can do to make them love you again. "I felt really alone. I felt really bitter. I felt sort of like a wounded animal lashing out."

During that period, she went through some difficult personal growth. "I had to deconstruct an entire belief system for my own personal sanity."

She started writing her sixth album, *Reputation*, which some critics call her darkest album. In *Miss Americana* she says it was also around that time that she fell in love with British actor Joe Alwyn. It was the first time she was truly happy without the external affirmation of the adoring crowd. She doesn't name Alwyn in the film and says they decided to keep their relationship quiet.

There were many other personal issues with superstardom Taylor had to overcome. As the world watched Taylor's every move, the woman who could have been a full-time fashion model if she weren't a singer, spent too much time looking in the mirror and listening to the body-shamers.

Miss Americana

In *Miss Americana*, Taylor reveals she had an eating disorder.

"I thought that I was just, like, supposed to feel like I was going to pass out at the end of a show or in the middle of it. I thought that's how it was. And now I realize no, if you eat food, have energy, you can get stronger, do all these shows, and not feel it."

> **Here's the SCOOP!** Taylor says she has rewired her brain to see that she's healthier and happier when she eats properly and doesn't scrutinize her body every day.

Now she doesn't freak out if someone says she looks like she's gained weight or speculates that she's pregnant because her stomach sticks out in a photo. A little extra weight means she's got curves and shinier hair, she wrote in an essay in *Elle*.

"The fact, that you know, I'm a size six instead

of a size double zero, I mean, that wasn't how my body was supposed to be, I just didn't really understand that. At the time I don't think I knew it."

She says she's figured out that it's impossible to meet every beauty standard. (Yes, it is!)

It also became impossible for Taylor to meet the standard of public behavior that her handlers and the country music world had drilled into her. She was always told to keep her mouth shut about politics. Look what happened to the Chicks, they would say. (See SCOOP! Extra on page 72 for more on the Chicks.) You'll lose fans if you dive into politics. So, she remained silent for years about her political beliefs. But she took a lot of heat for keeping mute on the 2016 presidential election. It was a case of you can't win no matter what you do.

But in 2018, during the midterm elections, she decided she couldn't keep quiet anymore. In *Miss Americana*, she talks about Marsha Blackburn, a Republican who was running for a Tennessee

State Senate seat. Blackburn, an ardent supporter of President Trump, voted against the reauthorization of the Violence Against Women Act and is not a supporter of LGBTQ rights—two issues that Taylor cares deeply about. Her father and people in her management team thought she shouldn't get involved in politics but she did, anyway.

Taylor says that after her sexual assault trial, she couldn't stand by and listen to people like Marsha Blackburn without reacting. If you don't know the details, this is what happened: Disc jockey David Mueller sued Taylor for $3 million, claiming that she had him wrongfully fired. Taylor countersued, for a symbolic one dollar, claiming that Mueller had groped her at a concert in 2013, and that's why he was fired. In 2017, the jury sided with Taylor. But she says the trial—which took place a few months before the Me Too movement started—was emotionally very difficult for her, and it made her think about all the women who have been sexually assaulted who don't have the platform she does—women who may not feel heard.

During the 2018 midterm elections, Taylor put up an Instagram post criticizing Blackburn and announcing she would vote for Blackburn's Democratic opponent Phil Bredesen, as well as the Democratic representative. And she asked that her fans educate themselves on the issues and register to vote. Blackburn won. But Taylor accomplished something pretty amazing: According to Vote.org, sixty-five thousand new voters registered in the twenty-four hours after her post. It was an unprecedented spike in voter registrations nationwide. Wow! That's some serious star power.

In *Miss Americana*, Taylor says it feels really good not being "muzzled" anymore. She acknowledges that she did it to herself. But it was the result of pressure from the people around her.

What has she realized from the experience? That she can be a pop singer and still be taken seriously in the political sphere. "I want to wear pink and tell you how I feel about politics. And I don't think those things have to cancel each other out."

There's a lot of pink and other bright colors in the *Lover* album and videos, and a dollop of political messaging, too. That's up next.

> **Here's a sartorial SCOOP!**
> **Taylor's light-up black sneakers, the "party shoes" she wears when she's doing vocal practice in *Miss Americana*, are by Pop and available on Amazon.**

SCOOP! EXTRA

THE CHICKS

The Chicks are comprised of sisters Martie MaGuire and Emily Strayer, and lead singer Natalie Maines. The band formed in Dallas in 1989, with a different lead singer. They were mostly doing bluegrass and country music and gained a wider following in 1998, when they hit it big with the album *Wide Open Spaces* and Natalie as their lead singer. They have made nine studio albums and have won thirteen Grammy Awards, and they're still performing. But they had a major bump in the road back in 2003. With a US-led coalition preparing to go to war with Iraq, the Chicks gave a concert in London. George W. Bush was the US president at the time. And the war was controversial. While they were introducing their song "Travelin' Soldier," Natalie Maines, who is from Texas, said, "Just so you know, we're on the good side with y'all. We do not want this war, this violence, and we're ashamed that the president of the United States is from Texas." The British audience cheered. But back home in the US, they were often ridiculed and worse. Some radio stations blacklisted them throughout the Bush administration, their albums were trashed in public protests, and talk shows and political pundits lashed out at them. The country music world did not treat the band kindly. The effect was chilling; their sales dropped, and they didn't tour again until 2010.

CHAPTER 8

LOVER

What's it like to release your seventh album? Apparently, it never gets old. On release day in August 2019, Taylor said she had Christmas vibes.

"You work on something for so long, and there's something about that anticipation before it comes out, just like going, what are they going to think of it?" she said on the Elvis Duran radio show.

> **Here's the SCOOP! Taylor says she likes the reaction videos fans make of themselves listening to her music. (noted)**

What does she think about *Lover*? "This album

is really a love letter to love, in all of its maddening, passionate, exciting, enchanting, horrific, tragic, wonderful glory," Taylor told *Vogue*. And it's the first album she's ever actually owned—which means nobody can sell it out from under her.

> **Here's the double SCOOP!**
> **When Big Machine Records was acquired by music producer Scooter Braun in 2019, Braun's company acquired the masters—or original recordings—of Taylor's first six albums. She was not happy.**

Following on the heels of *Reputation*, which she wrote in the aftermath of all that nastiness with Kanye and the Twitter masses, *Lover* definitely signals a change of heart that's palpable. She says it's like a new beginning, and it plays that way. Its title song tells you what you need to know about Taylor's current feelings on the subject of love.

She's all in, and it's sweet.

> Can I go where you go?
> Can we always be this close forever and ever?

"I've been thinking for years, God, it would just be so great to have, like, a song that people who were in love would want to dance to. Like slow dance to. In my head I had just like the last two people on a dance floor at 3 a.m., swaying," she said in a *New York Times* video interview. Check.

The song "Lover" has a dreamy late-night vibe that tells you her love with Joe Alwyn is grown-up and domestic, two people creating a home and life together. A snow globe (she does love Christmas) encasing a dollhouse of colorful retro rooms is the centerpiece of the video.

There are three videos for the album, and Taylor codirected all of them. The most colorful (although they're all loaded with color) and whimsical is for

"ME!" In *Miss Americana*, you see Taylor recording "ME!" with Brendon Urie (Panic! at the Disco). He's got a cold, but then he gets behind the mic and sounds fabulous, anyway. And Taylor explains what she's going for: a song that young kids can listen to, and think, I am the only person out there like me, and that's awesome. It's up-tempo and pure fun. The video starts off with a snake crawling along the ground that bursts into a bunch of rainbow butterflies—clearly a jab at Kim Kardashian and her followers calling Taylor a snake. But here she's saying enough with that—I'm going back to the things I love. Cue the cats.

Rolling Stone calls *Lover* Taylor Swift's "most epic" album. It's got more tracks than her other albums—eighteen. The magazine's review of *Lover* starts off with track seventeen, "It's Nice to Have a Friend," which isn't likely to get all that much attention. But it's a lovely, nostalgic song that takes Taylor back—and maybe the rest of us, too—to childhood, to the simplicity of early friendship.

> Lost my gloves, you give me one
> "Wanna hang out?" Yeah, sounds like fun

There's a lot about the *Lover* album that sounds like familiar Taylor; it's full of pop songs about love, many of them produced by Jack Antonoff, who makes a handful of appearances in *Miss Americana*, where we can see their longtime collaboration in action. Taylor will come in with partially finished lyrics . . . Antonoff will help her finish a phrase and lay down the beat.

In classic Taylor form, there are songs on this album that are clearly about specific people: It's not a stretch to say that "London Boy" is about Joe Alwyn, who, as noted before, is British.

But it's not all rainbows and fairy tales. On the sadder side is "Soon You'll Get Better," which is presumed to be about her mom's recurring cancer. The Chicks do backup vocals on that track.

"This is a wide-ranging emotional spectrum

that's on this album and that's why I love it so much," she told Elvis Duran.

One of the album's political tracks is "You Need to Calm Down," which lashes out at the anti-LGBTQ crowd.

> You just need to take several seats and try to restore the peace
> And control your urges to scream about all the people you hate
> 'Cause shade never made anybody less gay

The song has a dance beat, and the video is pure camp and features cameos by Ellen DeGeneres, RuPaul and a cadre of drag queens, Billy Porter, Laverne Cox, the *Queer Eye* guys, and Ryan Reynolds. And it ends with a message: She asks viewers to sign her petition to the Senate to support the Equality Act on Change.org.

Another track that could be called political is

"The Man." It's a catchy feminist anthem that asks if all the criticism leveled at her over the years would have been praise instead had she been a man. (Yup.) Here she sings about how much the media went after her for dating a series of famous men in her twenties.

> **They'd say I played the field before**
> **I found someone to commit to**
> **And that would be okay**
> **For me to do**
> **Every conquest I had made**
> **Would make me more of a boss to you**

Check out the video and stay until the very end. Mind blown!

Taylor talked to Elvis Duran about "The Man," and how she's wanted to write this song for a long time. She says there are specific words used to describe women's actions, and words with very different connotations to describe the same actions by men. For example: "A man does something strategic. A woman does the same thing, calculated. A man stands up for himself, a woman throws a tantrum. You can go on and on. A man is confident, a woman is smug."

Lover sounds like the beginning of a new phase for Taylor Swift. Not that the music is a departure from previous work or particularly new. But the songs, the lyrics, the messages ring with a new positivity and a new maturity. Hey, there are no accidents in Taylor Swift's music. The album ends with the song "Daylight."

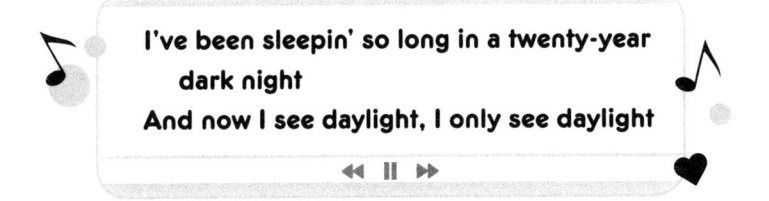

> I've been sleepin' so long in a twenty-year dark night
> And now I see daylight, I only see daylight

Sounds like Taylor is feeling good and looking to a bright future after some dark years. Does she look ahead twenty, thirty years? No, she told *CBS Sunday Morning*, because that puts her into

Scoop! Taylor Swift

a "panic spiral." But in the meantime, she's not taking a single day for granted. "It's actually really ungrateful to just assume that you have twenty years. Like, be stoked that you have today."

And in true T. Swift fashion, she surprised her fans and the music world by releasing her eighth studio album, *Folklore*, on July 24, 2020. The album was immediately praised by critics, and it even set a new record: most streams in a single day for a female artist on Spotify! What wasn't a surprise was that *Folklore* became Taylor's seventh consecutive number-one album in the US.

SCOOP! EXTRA

LOVER'S EASTER EGGS

Among the star's trademarks are her Easter eggs. There are tons of them in *Lover*. Here are a few to look for:

> "I Forgot That You Existed"—She writes, "In my feelings more than Drake," which is a reference to his hit song, "In My Feelings." Remember, she wore a Drake pin in that 2019 *Entertainment Weekly* cover profile.

> "Cruel Summer"—There's a line: "Devils roll the dice, angels roll their eyes," which is the name of a board game in the "Lover" video.

> "Lover" video—There's also a board game called King of Hearts in the video, like the song "King of My Heart" from *Reputation*.

"The Man" video—When the man makes a pit stop on the subway, he's at 13th Street, her lucky number. Graffitied on the wall are the names of some of her albums: *Reputation*, *Red*, *1989*, *Speak Now*, and *Fearless*, spelled backward. And the picture of the scooter crossed out is a reference to Scooter Braun, who now owns her master recordings.

"The Archer"—Taylor says track five is traditionally a vulnerable, personal song. There are arrows all over the "ME!" video, and in the "You Need to Calm Down" video, her friend Hayley Kiyoko shoots an arrow into a bull's-eye that's got a big ole number five on it.

"I Think He Knows"—We think she's talking about Joe Alwyn. Check out the reference to "indigo eyes." Joe's are blue.

"You Need to Calm Down" video—There's a cat face on a watch, a back tattoo of a snake turning into butterflies, and a phone case that spells out "Lover." And Ellen gets a tattoo from Adam Lambert that says, "Cruel Summer."

"ME!" video—Another snake turns into a swarm of butterflies, this time as the video starts.

SCOOP! QUIZ

HOW WELL DO YOU KNOW YOUR *LOVER*?

1. These lyrics are in what *Lover* song? "And baby, I get mystified by how this city screams your name. And baby, I'm so terrified of if you ever walk away."

   Long Live

2. What two items does Brendon Urie try to give Taylor before he gives her a kitten in the "ME!" video?

   flowers and a ring

3. Who is speaking about driving around on his scooter at the start of "London Boy"?

   _____

Scoop! Taylor Swift

4. Which Olympic figure skater appears in the video for "You Need to Calm Down"?

Adam rippon

5. "I dress to kill my time" are lyrics from what song?

Deth by a

6. What month are they going to take down the Christmas lights in the song "Lover"?

January

7. Finish the title of this song: "Miss Americana & the _and the hart drake prince_"

8. What actor from *Modern Family* appears in the "You Need to Calm Down" video?

Jesse Tyler Ferguson

9. Which famous actor is referenced in "The Man"?

Leonardo Dicapria

Lover

How did you do?

1-3 correct: Take your scooter and go.

4-7 correct: You may have some potential.

8-9 correct: You're The Man!

Check your answers on page 95!

SCOOP! QUIZ

THE ULTIMATE TAYLOR SWIFT QUIZ ⬇

1. Which Taylor body parts are double-jointed?

Her elbows

2. What fashion company did Taylor model for when she was a tween?

_____

3. What famous rocker was Taylor singing with when critics said she was off-key?

Stevie nicks

4. What song are these lyrics from: "Oh, it's so sad to think about the good times"?

Bad blood.

Lover

5. What nickname does Taylor use for her mom?

worst case in aro

6. Which Taylor Swift song earned a Guinness World Record for fastest-selling digital single?

We are never geting back to gether

7. What is Taylor's lucky number?

_13 ♡_

8. What is Taylor's favorite holiday?

christmas

9. What was Taylor's second album called?

Fearless

10. What song are these lyrics from: "She wears short skirts, I wear T-shirts"?

you be long whith me

Scoop! Taylor Swift

11. With whom did Taylor record the song "Best Days of Your Life"?

Kellie pickler

12. What is the name of Taylor's character in the film *Valentine's Day*?

felicia

13. How many Grammys has Taylor Swift won?

_10_

14. What song are these lyrics from: "But I got smarter, I got harder in the nick of time"?

Look what you made me do

15. On what album is the song, "Welcome to New York"?

_1989_

Lover

16. What is written on the fretboard of Taylor's guitar in the video for "Fifteen"?

Taylor

17. What song did Taylor write for the film *Cats*?

Beauitful gost

18. Whom did Taylor play in *Hannah Montana: The Movie*?

_on_

19. Which artist covered the entire *1989* album?

Taylor swift

20. What is the name of Taylor's third album?

speak now

Scoop! Taylor Swift

21. What kind of surgery did Taylor have in 2019?

Lasik eye surgery

22. Who was Taylor's first kiss when she was fifteen?

A boy named Drew

23. What underwater sea creature is Taylor afraid of?

sea urachen

24. One of Taylor's relatives was an opera singer. Who was it?

Hear grandmother

Lover

25. What song are these lyrics from: "And my daddy said, 'Stay away from Juliet'"?

Love Story

26. Who does the song "London Boy" reference?

Joe Alwyn

27. What does Taylor use for a microphone in the "You Belong With Me" video?

hair brush

28. In the "Mean" video, what is the waitress saving money for?

college

Scoop! Taylor Swift

29. The lyrics "The lights are so bright but they never blind me" are from what song?

Welcome to new York

30. In the video for "The Man," what does it say under the word "missing" on the subway sign?

if found return to Taylor swift

Scoring:

**1–10 correct answers:
No comment.**

11–20 correct answers: You're not getting any Secret Session invites just yet.

21–30 correct answers: Congratulations! You're a real-life certified Swiftie!

ANSWER KEY
♥ ♥ ♥

MATCH THE LYRICS TO THE *FEARLESS* SONG TITLES
1. "Breathe," 2. "Fearless," 3. "Fifteen," 4. "The Best Day," 5. "Hey Stephen," 6. "Love Story," 7. "Forever & Always," 8. "White Horse," 9. "Tell Me Why," 10. "You Belong With Me"

TAYLOR SWIFT, FEATURING . . .
1. "Long Live," 2. "Safe & Sound," 3. "I Don't Wanna Live Forever," 4. "End Game," 5. "The Last Time," 6. "ME!," 7. "Exile," 8. "Everything Has Changed," 9. "Bad Blood," 10. "Lover"

HOW WELL DO YOU KNOW YOUR *LOVER*?
1. "Cornelia Street," 2. Flowers and a ring, 3. Idris Elba, 4. Adam Rippon, 5. "Death by a Thousand Cuts," 6. January, 7. Heartbreak Prince, 8. Jesse Tyler Ferguson, 9. Leonardo DiCaprio

THE ULTIMATE TAYLOR SWIFT QUIZ
1. Her elbows, 2. Abercrombie & Fitch, 3. Stevie Nicks, 4."Bad Blood," 5. Worst-case scenario Andrea, 6."We Are Never Ever Getting Back Together," 7. 13, 8. Christmas, 9. Fearless, 10. "You Belong With Me," 11. Kellie Pickler, 12. Felicia, 13. 10, 14. "Look What You Made Me Do," 15. *1989*, 16. Taylor, 17. "Beautiful Ghosts," 18. Herself, 19. Ryan Adams, 20. Speak Now, 21. LASIK eye surgery, 22. A boy named Drew, 23. Sea urchin, 24. Her grandmother, 25. "Love Story," 26. Joe Alwyn, 27. Hairbrush, 28. College, 29. "Welcome to New York," 30. "If found, return to Taylor Swift"

HELP US PICK THE NEXT ISSUE OF

SCOOP!

HERE'S HOW TO VOTE:

Go to

www.ReadScoop.com

to cast your vote for who we should SCOOP! next.